Adso The Gull Who Quacked

By John G. Manuel
Illustrated By Ruth O'Neill

My heartfelt thanks to Kay for giving me the confidence to persist in publishing this book.

I am deeply grateful to Ruth O'Neill for bringing Adso to life through her beautiful illustrations.

Dedication

For all the children who are told they're different—remember, it doesn't matter. Just be yourself.

About the Author

After a lifetime of work in the Civil Service, I am now retired and enjoy spending much of my time reading. This story was inspired by a desire to help children and their parents understand that being different should never hold them back.

The wind that night was stronger than usual and whistled through the rafters and stanchions of the old iron bridge. Under the bridge, the ducks' nest rocked gently back and forth among the pile of reeds on the water in the reed bed. In the rafters on the bridge, the seagulls' nest was taking a battering, and slowly it began to tilt and tip. The three eggs inside the nest rolled to and fro, and eventually, one fell over the edge of the nest.

Down it tumbled, the cold water of the river beckoning below in the soft lights of the boats moored alongside the harbour jetty. The egg landed on the spongy reed mass by the side of the ducks' nest and then rolled gently into place among the four duck eggs inside.

The mother duck returned soon after to her nest, having washed the grime of a day's sitting away from her plumage, and although there was one more egg that looked a bit different, she nestled down to keep them warm as the storm began to grow; you see, ducks can't count, so five eggs were no different to four!

She sat on the eggs for another five days, and as she did, she quacked and murmured to them, and listened as the peeps and cheeps came back from inside. On the sixth day, four hatched, and yellow fluffy chicks emerged. The duck quacked reassuringly to them, and they nestled under her breast. She gently nudged the one remaining egg, and quacked to it, and she heard a cheeping back, so she settled down again to keep it and her chicks warm.

The following day, the last egg cracked, and out came an odd-looking bundle of down, and although it didn't look like the other four, it cheeped the same and smelt of her, so she named it Adso and cuddled it close under her wings with all the rest. Later, she led her chicks out of the nest and into the shallow water among the reeds by the nest. Four of her chicks loved the water and floated happily with each other, but the odd-looking one just stood up to his knees and shivered and shook and began to cry.

Thinking he would catch a cold, she went over and made him climb onto her back and nestle down between her wings, where he was warm and dry as she led the others out onto the water to swim and dabble among the reeds.

As they grew together, the five chicks quacked away and played among the reeds and shallows. Four were happy in the water, but Adso stayed on the bank or in the shallows. His brothers and sisters teased him about his dislike of the water, but it was only friendly teasing, and they always made sure he was included in their games. He grew up laughing and loving them. It wasn't the only thing they teased him about, though, as he preferred to eat insects and worms on the bank, and although he ate the greens that his mother gave him, he didn't really like seaweed and moss.

The nights began to get longer, and as they did,
Adso's down turned to speckled brown feathers, and
he began to look more like his brothers and sisters.
They were proper feathers too, so he was soon able
to join them on the water, splashing and playing and
chasing and shouting, although his quacks sounded
more like quarks!

One day, he was sitting on a fence post in the water
with one leg tucked underneath him (he liked to sit
on the post because his brothers and sisters didn't
seem to be able to land on it quite like he could; they
always fell off as they tried to stop in the air). He
saw two snowy white birds floating by below him in
the river, and although they weren't quacking, he
found that he could hear what they were saying to
each other. He quarked at them in excitement, but
was surprised when they looked at him in shock, and
one of them said to the other, 'Ugh, how common,
what on earth does he think he is?' And they flew off.

He spent his time dabbling with the other ducks, and as he talked to them, he began to understand that they, too, found him a little different. One day, when he was sitting on his post again and the wind was blowing hard, he felt the need to spread his wings. As he did so, he lifted off and soared up above the river and the reed beds into the sky where he floated along without having to flap. He quarked excitedly to his brothers and sisters below and told them to come and join him, but they quacked back that flying was too hard, and besides, he was getting awfully high and should watch what he was doing.

Adso soared higher and higher, never flapping his wings, and as he floated along, he drifted away from the river and over the salt marshes with their open spaces and meandering watercourses. He looked below him and saw hundreds of white dots against the green, and as he watched, they all began to shimmer and move at the same time.

Gradually, they got bigger and bigger, and soon he was
surrounded by gulls gliding on the breeze
like he was doing.

He quarked, 'Hello,' to the nearest of them, but it
just looked at him oddly and glided away. Next came a
gaggle of three squawking excitedly to each other
about how good the wind was for gliding and how well
they had eaten on the fish in the marshes that
morning. Adso quarked his agreement, but the gulls
ignored him. 'Hey, I'm talking to you,' he quarked, but
the gulls ignored him again. One turned to another
and said, 'What did he say? I didn't understand a
word.' The other gull replied, 'I don't know, he must
be one of those birds from up in the Arctic; they
speak a different language, don't they?' The third gull
squawked, 'Sounds more like a duck if you ask me.'
Adso quarked, 'That's it, that's right, I'm a duck!' The
three gulls looked at him again, shook their heads, and
flew away.

Adso glided down to his fence post once more and watched his brothers and sisters squabbling in the reeds and shallows, and pondered once more about himself.

The next day, very early before the sun rose, he flew towards the marshes again. He stayed low this time, gliding along the hedgerows and banks of the watercourses. As he flew along a bank with the water moving sluggishly below, he suddenly saw a brief flash of red amongst the bushes. Curious, he circled around and climbed a little higher, and as he returned, he saw that it was a fox. It was settled low among the bushes, staring intently at the green open marshland only feet away. Adso looked too, and there he saw a group of white gulls all sleeping on one leg with their heads folded back into their wings on their backs.

Adso was alarmed, and as he circled back once more, he watched the fox creep slowly and stealthily closer and closer in the bushes. What could he do? He flew low over the bushes where the fox was hiding and quarked a warning as he passed overhead, but none of the gulls took any notice, apart from the odd one that opened an eye to look at him before going back to sleep.

Adso watched the fox; it was preparing to pounce. He panicked and, closing his wings, zoomed right over the gulls on the grass, and as he went, he opened his beak, and suddenly he heard a squawking shout of 'Run, look out, look out!' coming from deep inside him. He shouted and shouted, and as he did so, all of the gulls rose into the air like snowflakes going upwards. The fox pounced at the nearest gull as it took off, but missed.

The gulls rose towards him, circling and swooping down around him, and he heard them shouting, 'Thanks, you saved us!' and 'Well done, youngster, well done!' and other different congratulations, and he understood everything that they said to him, and he was talking back to them too. It all came out a little oddly and sounded strange with quarks and squawks mingled together, but they understood him, and he understood them. Adso flew with them all day. He was very happy, but as the night began to draw in, he turned away and flew back to his post by the bridge and the reed beds.

He landed by his mother and quarked his story to her; she listened and smiled at him, and when he said, 'How can I understand these other birds as well as you and the others?' she paddled over to him and told him to follow her into the harbour. Together they swam towards one particularly big and shiny boat, with lots of gleaming chrome on its sides.

In the harbour lights, his mother said, 'Look, Adso, look at us and tell me what you see.' Adso looked at their reflection in the chrome and said, 'I see you, and I see me.' She said to him, 'Look again, Adso, and tell me what we look like.' Again, he looked in the chrome, and this time his eyes opened with surprise. 'We...we aren't the same,' he said. His mother said, 'No, Adso, we aren't, are we? Because you are not a duck like me; you are now a beautiful white gull.'

Adso looked at himself again and began to feel frightened. He looked at his mother, and he looked in the mirror at himself, and he began to cry. 'But if I am a gull and you are a duck, then you aren't my mother,' he sobbed through tears.

His mother put her wings around him. 'Adso, my dear Adso,' she said. 'Do you remember when you were little, how you hated the cold water, but your brothers and sisters loved it? Do you remember how they teased you because of it? Do you remember how I carried you on my back to keep you warm and dry?'

Adso nodded, and a tear dripped into the water beside him. His mother continued, 'I knew you were different then, but I loved you for it, as I love you now. As I look at you now, you have a wonderful ability: you can speak duck and gull, and because of that, you will always be different. But being different isn't a bad thing; it is a gift that makes you who you are.'

Adso looked again at the image of himself and saw that he was the same as the snowy white gulls he had played with that morning. Then he looked at his mother and threw back his head and quarked and squawked with delight.

He hugged his mother with his long white wings, and together they swam back to the reeds and the river, and as they went, the wind began to rise and whistle through the rafters and stanchions of the old iron bridge.

www.ingramcontent.com/pod-product-compliance
Lightning Source LLC
Chambersburg PA
CBHW040844010826
48978CB00012BB/897